LONE HUNTER
AND THE CHEYENNES

LONE HUNTER

AND THE

CHEYENNES

By
Donald Worcester

Illustrations by Paige Pauley

A SUNDANCE BOOK

Texas Christian University Press • Fort Worth

Library of Congress Cataloging in Publication Data
Worcester, Donald Emmet, 1915–
Lone Hunter and the Cheyennes.

"A Sundance book."
Reprint. Originally published: Oxford : Oxford
University Press, 1957.
Summary: Captured by the Cheyennes, two Oglala Sioux
boys escape through a blizzard and are saved by a grizzly
bear.

1. Oglala Indians—Juvenile fiction.   2. Children's
stories, American.   [1. Oglala Indians—Fiction.
2. Indians of North America—Fiction.   3. Grizzly bear—
Fiction]   I. Pauley, Paige, ill.   II. Title.
PZ7.W8873Ld   1985   [Fic]   85-4746
ISBN 0-87565-018-X

Illustrations by Paige Pauley
Design by Barbara Jezek,
Whitehead & Whitehead

Contents

To Kevin and Carolyn

LONE HUNTER
AND THE CHEYENNES

1

Enemy Raiders

LONE HUNTER PUSHED ASIDE THE TEPEE FLAP and looked out at the silent Oglala camp. A fine layer of frost glistened over the prairie in the early morning light. Summer, my twelfth summer, is over, he thought, and all too soon. But when the Great Spirit sends frost, he's telling us to get ready for winter camp. I'm glad my Gray Pony is fat, for the winter months are long.

Gray Pony whinnied softly, and Lone Hunter hurried to pet his pony and turn him loose to graze with the herd at the edge of camp. He untied his father's war and buffalo ponies and watched them trot out of camp, ears laid back, teeth bared, nipping playfully at one another and squealing as if enraged. Lone Hunter smiled as he watched them go. They were restless, spirited animals; it was pleasant just to watch them play.

He thought again of the passing of summer. Each year it was the same. Now the tribe would separate into small bands of thirty or forty men under their own chiefs and travel many days across

the plains to the south, where they camped for the winter in sheltered valleys. Warm days would still follow before the first snowfall. The hard-working beavers would finish laying in their winter's supply of bark and then plunge down to their underwater homes before the ice formed a thick layer over the streams. Huge

grizzly bears would pad through the berry patches, tearing at the clusters of ripe fruit, filling their empty stomachs before curling up in their caves for the Long Sleep.

As he thought of the long days of inactivity of winter camp, Lone Hunter frowned. No more would he race over the prairie on his fleet Gray Pony. Like the bears and the beavers, the Oglalas must wait patiently for the snows to melt and ice to crash downstream, the Great Spirit's signal that spring had come once more. Only then could the Oglalas move out on to the plains again and wander happily northward after the buffalo. Lone Hunter shook his head; summer was all too short, and winter too long.

Lone Hunter pulled his soft buffalo robe tightly about his bare shoulders and watched the rising sun turn the frost to sparkling drops of water. Soon all of the Oglalas were up, rubbing their cold arms to warm them. His friend, Buffalo Boy, came out of his father's lodge, stretching and yawning. Lone Hunter joined him. Together they walked through the huge camp, watching the Oglala women place willow baskets and rawhide cases heavy with pemmican, dried buffalo meat, outside the lodges.

"Some of the bands are leaving this morning," said Lone Hunter. "Summer is over already."

They heard the sound of hoofbeats and hurried between the tepees, out of the way, as other boys drove pack ponies into the camp. The women caught the ponies and tied them to stakes near the tepees.

"My father says by noon ours will be the only band left here," said Buffalo Boy. "Our medicine men want to gather bark of the red willow for smoking. We'll stay a few days longer."

"When we go south to winter camp," said Lone Hunter, "all we can do is chip arrowheads and braid ropes and wait and wait. Bears are wise to sleep all winter. They don't miss anything. While we still have time, let's fill up on ripe berries like the bears do before the Long Sleep."

"I'm willing," replied Buffalo Boy. "We won't have much to eat but dried meat until spring."

Like warriors setting off on the war path they walked to their fathers' lodges and picked up rawhide ropes, bows and quivers of arrows, and pouches containing flint for making fire, which they fastened to their belts near their flint knives. No Oglala ventured far from camp without his weapons.

Walking toward the plains at the edge of the camp, they came to the pony herd. Gray Pony whinnied and trotted up to Lone Hunter. Buffalo Boy caught his pony, and together they rode to the northwest, to the edge of the mountains.

On a hilltop they stopped to look back at the camp, at the edge of the rolling plains. It was on a neck of land jutting out into a canyon, and cliffs surrounded it on three sides. Enemies could approach it from one side only. As long as many Oglala warriors were there, it was a safe place and easily defended. Lone Hunter watched the Oglala bands move out of the camp onto the plains and turn south toward winter camps far away. He stared long at the camp.

"I know what you're thinking, Lone Hunter. Our band is small, and our young warriors few. If a large war party attacks us after the others go, we couldn't escape down the cliffs. But raiders aren't likely to come out this late, when it's time for winter camp."

They turned and rode on into the foothills. Tying their ponies where the grass was thick they plunged happily into the underbrush where clusters of juicy ripe blackberries bent the vines with their weight. They ate their fill of blackberries, sour wild cherries, and tiny, sweet strawberries. Stretching out on their robes in the shade, they stared at the prairie below. Lone Hunter rolled over onto his back, clasped his hands beneath his head, and closed his eyes. A crow flew over them, cawing loudly. Lone Hunter sat up, for a cawing crow was a sign of trouble.

"What is it, Un-ci-xi-ca?" he asked the crow.

The crackling of brush nearby made both boys leap to their feet and sprint for the nearest saplings. Once safely perched on limbs halfway up the tree trunks, they looked around to see what made the noise.

"Can you see anything, Lone Hunter? It sounds like a herd of bulls."

"A grizzly bear, I think. See, there it comes now."

A bear waddled through the brush, pushing it aside with the ease of a buffalo bull. It caught their scent, where they had been lying on the grass, and stared up at them with near-sighted eyes, while its black nose twitched. The boys held their breath. Grizzlies were powerful, more dangerous than angry bulls. Only the bravest warriors dared hunt them. Any man who wore a necklace of bear's claws was a man loved by the Great Spirit, a man whose medicine was strong. Others left the grizzlies alone and kept out of their way. No one who enjoyed seeing the sun rise each morning bothered a grizzly bear. Besides, the grizzly was a favorite of the Grandfather, the Great Spirit of the Oglalas.

The bear looked at the boys, as if undecided. "Go on eating your berries, Rota War-ank-xica," Lone Hunter called. "We don't want to harm you." He clasped his hands before him in sign language for peace.

The grizzly stared at them a moment longer, then shook its enormous head and padded off to continue its feast. "Bears are good medicine for you, Lone Hunter," whispered Buffalo Boy. "The Grandfather made it understand your words." Lone Hunter smiled. They watched until the bear was gone, then slid down the trees and walked silently to an icy stream where beavers were working industriously at building their winter shelter and laying in a supply of bark for food.

"The beavers are busier than usual, Lone Hunter. You know what that means. We'll have a long winter and much snow. The beavers know." Lone Hunter nodded in agreement. Silently they squatted on the ground. An old beaver stood guard on the opposite bank, watching them, ready to slap the ground with its tail as a warning to the others at the first sign of danger.

The boys remained still, and the beavers continued floating the logs into place in their dam. Suddenly the old beaver slapped the earth with its tail and dived into the water.

"Listen!" said Lone Hunter. He lay down and placed his ear to the ground. "Horses or buffalo." He arose and together they ran up the hill, keeping in the underbrush, out of sight. At the top of the hill they knelt and pushed aside chokecherry branches. A small herd of wild horses galloped past them, from the direction of the Oglala camp.

"Wild horses," said Lone Hunter. "But what frightened them?"

"Maybe it's just the cool weather. Maybe they feel like running."

"No. The stallion was at the rear, guarding the mares and colts from danger. Someone frightened them. It wasn't Oglalas. We have plenty of meat so none of our hunters are out. Bad medicine! It may be Crows or Cheyennes or Assiniboines, trying to steal Oglala ponies."

"It may be," said Buffalo Boy, "but they should be preparing their winter camps. They usually don't raid this late in the summer."

They stood silently, scarcely breathing, straining their ears for sounds, but the wind was blowing from them toward the distant Oglala camp. Thick clusters of ripe berries were all around them, but they no longer thought of eating.

For a few moments longer they stayed at the hilltop, staring in the direction of the Oglala camp beyond the rolling plains. Lone Hunter rubbed his eyes, stared again, then leaped to his feet. Buffalo Boy, too, saw the tiny puffs of dark smoke rising skyward in the distance.

"Danger! The camp is attacked. They've signaled to the others for help."

They ran to their ponies, untied them, and sprang to their backs. Without urging, the ponies galloped toward the Oglala camp. Lone Hunter guided Gray Pony swiftly through ravines, to keep out of sight of the enemy war party. When they were near the camp, he pulled up and listened. Clearly he heard the shouts and war cries. The boys slipped off their ponies and tied them in a ravine. Dropping their robes, they crawled to the crest of the hill and peered over it. Beyond, in plain sight, was the Oglala camp.

"Eyah!" said Lone Hunter. "Cheyennes. A big party, with many more warriors than we have left in camp." The Oglalas had raced to the highest ground and piled up robes and rawhide cases full of pemmican to form a breastwork. The warriors crouched behind it, bows drawn, while the women and children were huddled together at the edge of the cliffs.

"Lone Hunter, look!" Buffalo Boy pointed to the plains to the south. Two smoke signals, far apart, rose in answer. "At least two of the bands are coming."

Lone Hunter watched the Cheyennes. One of their warriors, sitting his pony on high ground as a lookout, also saw the signal. He shouted to the war chief, who rode to join him. The Cheyennes drew in close around the chief, who pointed to the distant smoke signals and to the small group of Oglala warriors. Then the Cheyennes spread out in a long line and faced the Oglalas. They held war clubs in their right hands, and shields hung on their left arms. Lone Hunter choked, and for a moment could not speak.

"They're going to rush the camp," he said. "The others can't return in time to stop them. What can we do to delay them?"

The Cheyennes whooped loudly and held their shields in the

air above their heads. The chief faced them and sang his war song. Another sound arose above the shouts and war cries, a mournful, wailing sound. Lone Hunter bit his lip when he heard it. The Oglala warriors, determined to fight to the death to save their women and children, were singing their death songs.

II

Prairie Fire

LONE HUNTER STARED THROUGH THE DRIED buffalo grass at the huge war party of Cheyennes, massing for the attack. He glanced at Buffalo Boy and saw that his friend, too, was trying to think of some way to save their band. Lone Hunter looked at his bow, his knife, and touched the pouch at his belt. Nothing in it but flint for making fire. "Fire! That's it," he whispered. "The wind will blow it right at them, and they'll have to run for their lives. Before they have time to attack again, the other Oglalas will be near. Then our fathers will be saved."

"But, Lone Hunter, what will our people do when fire comes toward them?"

"They can make a backfire. Just a strip of burned grass will save them. They'll think of it. Let's hurry before we're too late."

They ran down to the ravine and turned the ponies loose, knowing that both animals would rejoin the Oglala herds. Quickly they tore loose bunches of dry grass to serve as torches, and searched for tinder. "I wish we could find some dry moss," said Buffalo Boy. "We'll have to use grass, and it's hard to light. You strike the sparks. I'll hold the grass and try to make it burn."

They knelt over the torches, and Lone Hunter drew from his pouch a jagged piece of flint and a rough stone. He held the flint over Buffalo Boy's cupped hands and struck it with the stone. When sparks flew into the grass, Buffalo Boy raised his hands and blew into them. A blade of grass glowed brightly for a moment, and a tiny curl of smoke arose. Buffalo Boy lowered his hands, to feed more grass on the fire. The leaf turned black, and the flame disappeared. Beyond the hill the war cries of the Cheyennes grew suddenly louder, drowning out the death chants of the Oglalas. "They're getting up courage for the attack," said Lone Hunter. He glanced about desperately for something to use as tinder.

Under his knee lay a withered milkweed plant, with its pointed seed pods open. Already the wind had scattered the seeds, with their white, fuzzy coverings. But one pod had been trampled deep into the grass, out of the wind. Lone Hunter seized it and pulled out the seeds. "Try this," he said, placing them in Buffalo Boy's hands. Again he struck sparks with flint and stone. They glowed brightly as Buffalo Boy blew on them, then burst into flame. The boys lighted their torches and raced across the prairie.

As they ran they paused from time to time to touch their torches to the dry grass near their feet. The wind whipped the flames violently, and the fire flew toward the Oglala camp and the line of Cheyenne warriors. The rumbling and crackling of the prairie fire rose above the shrill war cries of the Cheyennes, who paused in their advance. Lone Hunter saw them turn and whip their ponies in a mad race for the edge of the fire and safety.

Oglala warriors sprang over their crude barricade and built small fires between it and the raging flames. Lone Hunter merely glanced at them, for the Oglalas were used to sudden prairie fires and knew how to protect themselves by burning off the grass around them and stamping out the flames. Beyond the charred strip of grass they would be safe. But the Cheyennes, closer to the fire and mounted on their frightened war ponies, had no chance to build backfires. They could only flee for their lives, whipping their ponies at every stride.

Lone Hunter and Buffalo Boy watched until the fleeing Cheyennes reached safety beyond the edge of the flames, then they ran to the nearest ravine. They flung themselves into the thick grass among the whitened bones of a buffalo bull. Lone Hunter lay facing the huge skull, which seemed to stare at him from eyeless sockets.

"Help us, Ta-tan-ka," he whispered to the bull. "Make the Cheyennes return to their own lands. Don't let them find us."

Lone Hunter flattened himself against the ground, almost covered by the tall grass, and waited for the hoofbeats of the Cheyenne ponies to die out in the distance as they started for their own hunting grounds across the mountains. After an easy victory had been snatched from their hands the Cheyennes would be angry and eager for revenge. But they would have little time to search for Lone Hunter and Buffalo Boy before Oglala warriors came to the rescue and drove them away. The smoke signals had warned them other Oglalas were coming.

The hoofbeats of the Cheyenne ponies came nearer, and Lone Hunter suspected some warrior had seen them running for the ravine. He heard angry voices, and the words rattled like hailstones on a tepee, but he could not understand what they were

saying. He lay quietly, hoping the Great Spirit would make the
Cheyennes turn away. He heard them ride around the ravine,
then stop their ponies. He held his breath, though his lungs felt
as if they would burst.

A soft clicking sound drifted toward Lone Hunter's head.
What was that strange yet familiar sound? It was not Cheyenne
moccasins trampling the dried grass. He raised his head slightly.
A prairie rattlesnake, sluggish in the cool shade, slithered from
behind the bull's white skull, its rattles clicking softly against the
dry grass. Lone Hunter drew back as the snake came towards him
in its strange, looping way, ready to coil and strike at any moment. It feels my warmth, he thought. That's why it comes to me.

He hissed softly at the snake, to turn it away without frighten-
ing it, but still it came on. In desperation he snipped a seed pod at
it, striking its head. The snake coiled, its forked tongue darted
out, and behind its head its rattles vibrated angrily. Lone Hunter
backed an arm's length away, barely out of striking distance. The
snake continued to rattle. He heard the Cheyennes laugh.

We're lost, Lone Hunter thought. They heard the snake, and
they don't need to see me to know where I am. But if I go to
them now, maybe they won't find Buffalo Boy. He still has a
chance to escape.

Lone Hunter arose and walked around the angry rattlesnake to the steep bank. He crawled up the side of the ravine toward the Cheyennes, pulling himself up by holding on to bunches of grass. His heart pounded, and his mouth was dry. Near the top he paused and looked back at Buffalo Boy crouching in the grass, almost hidden from sight. He heard the stamping of the Cheyenne ponies and the guttural voices of the warriors. They were coming closer. In terror Lone Hunter looked about, but there was no escape. If he ran their arrows would pierce his back before he had gone five steps.

He pulled himself up to the top of the ravine and looked up at the nearest Cheyennes. Their angry faces scowled at him behind drawn bows, the bowstrings pulled back even with their ears. Lone Hunter gasped and swallowed hard. His legs trembled so he feared he would not be able to stand. As he pulled himself to his feet, he saw the Oglala camp and the smoke-tipped lodge of his father. Would he ever see it again? He forced his eyes away from the camp, drew himself up to full height, and walked steadily toward the scowling Cheyennes.

III

Captives

THE CHEYENNES GRUNTED IN SURPRISE AS LONE
Hunter approached them but held their short, heavy bows ready,
arrows resting on the taut bowstrings. The war chief lowered his
bow and spoke to the warriors. One of them replied loudly, wav-
ing two fingers. He must have seen both of us, Lone Hunter
thought. The others are not sure. What can I do to make them
forget Buffalo Boy?

He turned toward the Oglala camp while the Cheyennes ar-
gued. "Eyah!" he exclaimed, and pointed to the prairie far to the
south. Two dust clouds rose in the distance, as Oglala warriors
raced to answer the smoke signal, the call for help from the camp.

Seeing the returning Oglalas, the Cheyennes wheeled their

ponies. Still they did not start. The chief motioned to one of the warriors, who slipped from his pony's back and ran to the ravine. He returned in a few moments, holding Buffalo Boy by the arm. He pushed Buffalo Boy alongside Lone Hunter and looked at the chief.

"What shall we do, Lone Hunter? Do you think they'll kill us?"

"I don't know yet," Lone Hunter answered, without taking his eyes off the chief's face. "Don't let them know we're afraid. They'll surely kill us if they think we're cowards."

The two boys stood side by side, staring at the stern-faced warriors, concealing the fear that made their hearts pound like stampeding buffalo. The war chief drew his bow and leveled an arrow at Lone Hunter's chest, while another Cheyenne pointed his lance at Buffalo Boy and pulled back his arm as if to hurl it.

The boys held their breath but did not lower their gaze. After staring at them a moment, the Cheyenne chief grunted and lowered his bow. He spoke to the warriors and pointed to the captives. Two warriors lifted the boys to their ponies' backs and, holding them each by an arm, galloped towards the mountains.

"Maybe they're going to adopt us, not kill us," Lone Hunter called to Buffalo Boy above the drumming hoofbeats. "It depends on how we act."

The warrior holding Lone Hunter on his war pony shook his arm roughly as a signal for silence, and Lone Hunter said nothing more. They rode into the foothills toward the mountains, following a trail marked by fresh pony tracks. So this is the way the Cheyennes enter our hunting grounds, thought Lone Hunter.

As they traveled higher into the foothills toward the edge of the Oglala hunting grounds, Lone Hunter saw fewer and fewer familiar landmarks. Finally he looked about in terror and saw nothing at all that he recognized. It was strange country that lay between Oglala and Cheyenne hunting grounds.

The trail wound upward toward the mountain towering above

them. Lone Hunter's eyes raised to the rocky heights overhead. Even if they turned us loose I wouldn't know which way to go, he thought. I'm so scared I haven't even watched for landmarks I could recognize later. A fine warrior I'll make.

As he followed the twisting trail upward, Lone Hunter caught sight of Buffalo Boy's face. He's as frightened as I am, Lone Hunter thought. We might as well be learning this strange country as thinking about what the Cheyennes will do to us. Besides, it's a warrior's duty to know the country where he is, even on his last ride. My father has told me so many times.

He thought of his father, Red Eagle, and of their hunts together. He remembered the way his father had stopped and pointed out an unusual feature of a hill or a tree or a stone. "Remember what is different and unusual, my son," he had said. "That makes it easier. Always remember the unusual landmarks, for if you are riding for your life most hills and trees look alike. The sight of a hill or a tree you remember can save your life. I know you, my friend, you will say to it. Now I know where I am. Now I can escape. And remember, my son, a warrior must know enemy lands as well as his own. Learn the landmarks wherever you go. Mark them in your mind like the drawings on a tepee, never to fade."

With an effort Lone Hunter forced his mind from his father and back to the winding trail. He stared at the rocks, but they became blurred masses before his eyes. He shook his head, trying to clear his mind. The Cheyenne warrior riding in front of him on the same pony turned and stared at him. Lone Hunter looked down at the trail beneath the pony's hooves.

Crossing a stream, the Cheyennes let their ponies drink. For a few moments Buffalo Boy was alongside him, and Lone Hunter spoke softly. "Have you watched all the landmarks? Could you guide a war party through this country?"

Buffalo Boy looked surprised but said nothing, for the Cheyennes frowned at them. When they traveled on up the trail, Lone Hunter knew that Buffalo Boy would be straining to learn and remember the landmarks. He, too, concentrated on memorizing each prominent feature of the country and for a time almost forgot his fear of the Cheyennes. Even when darkness fell, he strained his eyes to make out the shapes of hills and the turns and bends of the trail.

On they climbed, not stopping to make camp until a thick, white band of little stars, the Ghost Trail, was high overhead. While one of the Cheyennes listened a few moments for sounds of pursuit, the others placed the boys among them so they could not move without disturbing some warrior, and rolled up in their robes to sleep. The mountain air was cold, and Lone Hunter wrapped his robe tightly about him. When he awoke in the morning, the wrinkles in his robe were white with frost.

Early in the morning, as they rode up the trail, the Cheyennes stopped to drink at an icy spring seeping out of brown cliffs on the side of the mountain above the foothills. Not far above the spring Lone Hunter saw the black opening of a cave in the rock. Scattered before the mouth of the cave were the bones of animals. A bear's cave, he thought. It must be nearly time for the Long Sleep. As he watched, a gigantic grizzly bear waddled out of the cave and sniffed the wind that bore the scent of the intruders. The bear stared at them a moment with its near-sighted eyes, then bared its teeth and started toward them. Lone Hunter held up his hands clasped together before him. "Go back, Rota War-ank-xica," he called.

The Cheyennes followed Lone Hunter's gaze to the bear. They

mounted hastily, and two warriors pulled the boys up behind them. Their ponies could not outrun the bear on the rough mountain trail, and if it charged them it would surely kill some of the ponies. Their whips cracked on the ponies' moist flanks as they sped up the trail. The bear watched them go, shaking its great head, then reentered the cave. Lone Hunter saw Buffalo Boy and the Cheyennes staring at him. They think it's my medicine that kept the bear from chasing us, he thought.

They rode all day, crossing the summit through a narrow pass between enormous boulders. Lone Hunter looked left and right along the mountain top, which rose higher than the pass in either direction. Huge boulders with sharp peaks jutting out among

them marked the top of the mountain. Anyone who missed the narrow pass would spend days trying to climb through and around and over the peaks and boulders. We must never forget this pass or how to find it, Lone Hunter thought.

The trail down the mountain was over loose shale and poorly marked. In vain Lone Hunter searched for some easily recognizable landmark to show that the pass was near. The whole mountainside, as far as he could see in either direction, looked the same. Nothing but loose shale and a few scattered pines and firs could be seen. From the valley floor, where the Cheyennes made camp, he could not even see the pass where the trail crossed the mountain.

Lone Hunter looked up toward the summit, following with his eyes the faint trail as it wound back and forth, higher and higher. It's easy to follow the trail now, he thought, but how would it look if the mountain was covered with snow? Even a good warrior might not take the right direction to the pass.

A short way up the mountain and near the trail was a huge pine with gnarled limbs, a pine that looked like many others on the mountainside. An evening wind blew through the tree, and the twisted limbs made a murmuring sound, like two or three people humming or talking. Cold and hungry, Lone Hunter rolled up in his robe and listened to the murmuring voices of the pine. He thought of his father's lodge and the voices of Oglalas heard faintly in the dark. Closing his eyes tightly, he pulled his robe around his ears to drown out the sound.

On the third morning they crossed the last mountain and followed the trail down past huge red cliffs streaked with brown and deep canyons cut by icy streams from the snowbanks above. The land near the foot of the mountain was heavily wooded, but beyond Lone Hunter saw open hilly grasslands crossed by streams thick with alders and firs. He glanced to the north and south along the mountain. As far as he could see in either direction were cliffs and canyons.

A short ride from the mountain the Cheyennes stopped by a stream to drink and rest before riding on. Across the stream was a sheer cliff of gray rock streaked with black and red. Lone Hunter looked up to the top of the cliff, where it tapered off to a sharp peak. In dim light it could easily be mistaken for a tepee. Here was the first landmark easy to recognize.

As they approached the Cheyenne camp the warriors stopped once more. A scout rode his pony to the top of a hill and watched them, a scout from the Cheyenne camp. The chief signaled to him that the war party had returned without loss of a man and with enemy captives. The scout relayed the message to the Cheyenne camp. Lone Hunter and Buffalo Boy watched the signals and understood them easily, for the sign language was known to all the tribes of the northern plains.

Another scout from the Cheyenne camp rode up with a deer across his pony's back. The warriors dismounted and built a fire. They want to give the camp time to prepare for their return, Lone Hunter thought. He and Buffalo Boy watched hungrily while the warriors devoured the half-cooked venison. When all had eaten and nothing remained but well-cleaned bones, the war party mounted again. The chief led the way at a gallop. The others whooped loudly and followed, racing into the camp as if charging the enemy. Everyone in the camp came out to meet them, shouting and singing. Cheyenne boys glared at Lone Hunter and Buffalo Boy and drew their fingers across their throats, the sign for Sioux. When the warriors dismounted, they went to one side to talk, while a crowd of stony-faced women surrounded the two Oglala prisoners.

The angry women surged in closer. Lone Hunter held his breath. He wanted badly to run for his life, to leave the Cheyennes far behind, but there was no escape. They want us to run, he thought. Then they will club us to death. Instead of running, he looked from one face to another, trying hard to hide his fear.

"What do you think they'll do, Lone Hunter?"

"I don't know. I think the warriors are trying to decide whether to keep us or kill us. They may think we're too old to make good Cheyennes now, that we won't be able to forget our own people. I hope they decide to adopt us. Then at least we will be alive. But these women are thinking of sons and brothers killed by Oglalas. They want us killed."

The chief who led the war party glanced at the women moving closer to the boys, left the warriors, and pushed his way through the crowd. He took Lone Hunter and Buffalo Boy by an arm and led them into a tepee. Leaving them alone in the lodge, he went outside once more.

Lone Hunter peered out through a small opening at the side of the tepee flap and saw a Cheyenne warrior standing guard. Women and boys stood in a semicircle before the lodge, waiting for word from the chief.

"I'd rather become a Cheyenne than be killed," said Lone Hunter. "I wonder what it would be like to forget our own people and live always with the Cheyennes? You remember Gray Hawk; he was captured from the Cheyennes while a young boy. Now he's just like other Oglalas. He doesn't even remember the Cheyennes. And Raven. He's forgotten the Assiniboines, who once were his people. Maybe that will happen to us, if they decide to keep us. I'm sure I could never forget my father and mother, and my Gray Pony. Still, it would be better than being filled with Cheyenne arrows. We might even have a chance to escape some time."

Buffalo Boy raised his head. "Escape," he said. "Do you really think we might?"

Lone Hunter stared through the narrow slit. Suddenly his

body stiffened, and he felt Buffalo Boy stir uneasily at his side. "They're through talking," he said. "They've decided. The chief is telling the women."

Lone Hunter hurried away from the tepee entrance, and squatted on a robe, with Buffalo Boy beside him. "Let's pretend to be looking at the paintings on the tepee covering," he said. "Here's a bow and arrows and a war club within reach. If they're coming to kill us, take the war club and hold them off while I string the bow. At least we can die like Oglalas."

They looked up at the drawings of horses and buffalo in green and red and black paints. Lone Hunter wiped his moist hands on the robe. Why don't they hurry? He heard the tepee flap being raised.

The war chief crouched at the tepee entrance, looking in at the two boys. Lone Hunter and Buffalo Boy slowly turned their heads to see him, ready to spring to their feet. "He's not coming in," Lone Hunter whispered. "It looks bad for us. He'll probably try to get us to come outside. Be ready."

Out of the corner of his eye Lone Hunter saw the bow and quiver hanging near his hand. It would take but a moment to string the bow. If Buffalo Boy could keep the Cheyennes from rushing in . . .

The chief entered the tepee quickly and stood in the center for a moment, tall and terrifying. Lone Hunter licked his dry lips. Now there was no chance to fight. They had waited too long.

The chief held up his hands, and pointed to Lone Hunter, then to Buffalo Boy. Holding one arm out before him, he made slashing motions across it with his other hand. Lone Hunter leaped to his feet.

"Striped arrows! Sign language for Cheyennes," he said. "They're going to keep us."

IV

Snowbound

TWO CHEYENNE WOMEN CAME INTO THE TEPEE, and the chief went out. When he saw they were smiling, Lone Hunter relaxed and sat again on the robe. "These must be our new mothers," he said. "We must make them like us. They must think we're happy staying with them. If they believe that, we may have a chance to escape before we forget our own people."

The Cheyenne women handed each of the boys a large piece of broiled venison and sat beside them, watching them eat. As he tore ravenously at the venison, Lone Hunter glanced at the woman by his side. She smiled and pointed to herself, then touched a blue feather. In the same motion she made the sign for night—earth covered over—and bent her thumb and finger in the sign for star. Lone Hunter put down the meat. "Blue Star," he said. She pointed at him.

He held up one finger, making the sign for alone, then held his right hand, palm out, near his shoulder, pointing two fingers up like the ears of a wolf, the plains sign for hunter. The woman laughed and spoke in Cheyenne.

Lone Hunter turned to Buffalo Boy. "Her name is Blue Star," he said, pointing to the Cheyenne woman beside him.

"Hers is Rainbow Woman," said Buffalo Boy, pointing to the other. The two Cheyenne women smiled and continued talking in sign language. They had no sons, they said. Their husbands had not come back from raids, and they were alone. They were happy to have fine sons at last, sons who one day would supply meat and hides for their lodges and ponies to carry their possessions.

When the boys finished eating, Rainbow Woman beckoned to Buffalo Boy to follow and left the tepee. Lone Hunter arose and watched from the tepee entrance to see where they went. They don't want us to be together, he thought. They're probably afraid if we're together we'll try to escape. Blue Star came and stood beside him.

As Buffalo Boy and Rainbow Woman walked to another tepee, they passed a young warrior. He turned and scowled at Buffalo Boy, brandishing his flint knife. Blue Star pulled Lone Hunter back into the tepee. By signs she told him the warrior's name, Two Elks. She explained that he hated Oglalas more than all other tribes, for his brother had been killed on a raid against them. He would watch for them to try to escape or for any opportunity to kill them.

Other Cheyennes who lived in the tepee came in, two couples and a boy. They sat on their robes and spoke to Blue Star, nodding their heads toward Lone Hunter. He looked at the small fire in the center of the lodge, afraid to face them. Perhaps they, like Two Elks, wanted no Oglalas among them. When they stopped talking, Lone Hunter examined the Cheyenne lodge. It was beautifully made, like those of the Oglalas. Near the outer rim were the rawhide cases full of pemmican for winter, and willow baskets for the families' possessions. The dress of the Cheyennes, he noticed, was also like that of the Oglalas, and they, too, wore

their hair in two braids. He saw nothing unusual in the lodge except two strange pieces of curved wood hanging from a stake. Rawhide strands were woven between the curves, and loose thongs hung down.

At dark Lone Hunter rolled up in his robe, but sleep did not come easily. He lay still, so the Cheyennes would think he slept. He thought of his father, mourning the loss of his only son, and of his mother. By now she must have cut off her hair and gashed her arms and legs in grief. He thought of Gray Pony and imagined the pony watching for him to come, morning after morning, whinnying for him in vain. A lump rose in his throat. We must escape, he thought. There must be some way. But how?

In the morning Lone Hunter walked through the Cheyenne camp. The tepees were set up in two circles, one within the other, unlike the long, irregular lines of Oglala tepees. He wandered aimlessly to the edge of the camp, beyond which were dense woods. A Cheyenne warrior mounted on a swift pony rode out of the woods and strung his bow. It was Two Elks. Lone Hunter returned to the center of the camp.

The war chief who had led the raid against the Oglalas came from his tepee and beckoned to Lone Hunter. By signs he told Lone Hunter to call Buffalo Boy. When the two boys were together, the chief spoke to them in sign language.

"My sons," he said, "some of our people don't want you because you are Oglalas. If you leave camp alone for any reason they may kill you. If you try to escape they will follow you till they catch you, to bring back your scalps. Stay in camp and learn our language. In time they will forget. It is not good that they see you together often."

The chief walked away. Lone Hunter and Buffalo Boy stood together a few moments longer. "If we could be together, Lone Hunter, I wouldn't mind it so much."

"Let's try to meet once each day, for just a short time. A little before sundown will be the best time, for that is when we think too much about our own people. Think every day of some way to escape. We must find a way that won't fail, for those who follow won't bring us back alive."

They parted. I wonder if Buffalo Boy feels like I do, Lone Hunter thought. I want to lie on my robe and never move again. But I must not do that, or we'll never escape.

He returned to the lodge and sat by the Cheyenne boy, making signs to ask him his name. It was Brave Elk.

Brave Elk seemed reluctant to talk with Lone Hunter, but when Lone Hunter signaled that he had heard the Cheyenne ponies were the best of any tribe, Brave Elk leaped to his feet. He beckoned to Lone Hunter to follow and led the way to the edge of the camp. There in a grassy valley, on the opposite side of the camp from the woods, was an enormous pony herd, almost as large as that of the Oglalas.

The two boys sat on the top of a knoll, while Brave Elk pointed out famous war and buffalo ponies and named the tribes from which they had been taken. Lone Hunter recognized some Oglala ponies, and Brave Elk showed him others taken from the Crows and Pawnees. The Cheyennes had many fine ponies, but they guarded them well. The best animals were herded all day and tied at night by their owners' lodges. While the two boys sat on the hill, Brave Elk taught Lone Hunter the Cheyenne words for ponies, tepees, bows and arrows, and fire.

Two days later the air turned bitterly cold, and the ground was frozen. Dark clouds hid the sun. Snow had not yet fallen, but winter had come. At a signal from the Dog Soldiers, the camp police, the women packed their possessions and took down the lodges. Like the Oglalas they tied the lodge poles on each side of the pack ponies, crossing the forward ends over the ponies' heads and letting the other ends drag on the ground. Behind the ponies' heels they tied willow baskets. When these travois were packed, the Dog Soldiers signaled again, and the camp moved.

Lone Hunter and Buffalo Boy walked all day with Blue Star and Rainbow Woman, helping them carry their few possessions, for they had no ponies. The other couples living with them carried the tepee poles and coverings on their few ponies. Late in the afternoon they stopped in a sheltered valley where grass was heavy and cottonwood trees thick. The women set up the tepees and built cook fires.

In the morning the Cheyennes separated into small bands and all but one of them struck their tepees and moved on. Only fifty lodges were left in the camp.

"Where are they going?" Lone Hunter asked Brave Elk.

"They'll make camps in other valleys," he replied. "There aren't enough cottonwood trees here to feed all the ponies when the snow covers the grass."

Each day Lone Hunter watched the pony herd, looking for the swiftest animals, and at night he saw where they were tied. One evening just after sundown, he walked through the camp, thinking of some way to steal ponies and escape across the mountains before the snows blocked the trail. At one lodge he saw six splendid ponies and stopped to admire them.

A Cheyenne warrior stepped from the shadows. Lone Hunter barely choked down his terror. The warrior was Two Elks. Slowly he raised his right hand and drew his finger across his throat, then gave the sign for lifting a scalp. Lone Hunter walked away, resisting the urge to run for his life, the skin on his back writhing in dread of a thrust of Two Elks' knife. Two Elks is still waiting and watching, he thought, hoping we will try to escape. When we do he will be ready, and if we fail our scalps will soon be hanging before his lodge.

Lone Hunter did not go near Two Elks' lodge again, and whenever he saw the Cheyenne warrior in camp, he tried to avoid him.

But now that the camp was small, this was not easy. Each time he saw the angry warrior, it seemed that the man's hatred for Oglalas had increased. One day, thought Lone Hunter, one day he'll kill us right here in camp, and no one will be able to stop him.

Brave Elk, too, was worried. "You must watch out for Two Elks," he said. "He swears he'll kill you both before the snows melt in the spring, even if you don't try to escape."

The days grew shorter and the nights longer, and one morning Lone Hunter awoke to see the mountains covered with a blanket of snow. Yellow Bear, Brave Elk's father, called to him. He held his hands closed before his body, then pointed his fingers down. Rain. Opening his hands flat, he made a sweeping motion right and left, to indicate snow lying on the ground. Then he held his hands above his head and pointed to the mountain passes, dimly seen in the cloudy air. Lone Hunter looked at the white mountains and understood. The snow in the passes lay deeper than a man's head. No one could cross the mountains now, for ponies would flounder helplessly in the deep drifts. Escape was impossible.

V

Flight

WARM DAYS FOLLOWED, AND THE SNOW MELTED
except for a strip at the crest of the mountains. "It's safe for us to
be together more now, Lone Hunter," said Buffalo Boy. "Only
Two Elks hasn't forgotten that we're Oglalas. The others no
longer watch us, since they know we can't escape."

The sky grew dark with clouds once more, and a fresh blanket
of snow fell heavily on the camp. Even when the snow had
stopped falling the sky remained overcast. With Brave Elk the two
boys walked to the meadow and watched the ponies pawing
through the snow to reach the grass underneath.

Brave Elk pointed to the dark sky. "Coldmaker is coming with
more snow," he said in Cheyenne, at the same time making signs

so Lone Hunter and Buffalo Boy would understand. "Soon we'll have to break cottonwood branches to feed the ponies." Lone Hunter looked at the slow-moving clouds and at the tree limbs sagging beneath the weight of the snow. More snow was coming, there was no doubt of that. He thought of the bleak mountain passes, buried under deep snowdrifts, and frowned.

They walked back to the camp, their moccasins wet in the soft snow. Some Cheyenne hunters came out of the camp toward them. They walked in a curious, waddling fashion, but moved swiftly over the snow. Lone Hunter and Buffalo Boy stopped and watched. On the hunters' feet were curved pieces of wood with rawhide thongs woven across them, like the ones they had seen hanging on a stake in Yellow Bear's tepee.

"What do they have on their feet?" Lone Hunter asked Brave Elk, pointing to the warriors' tracks in the snow. Brave Elk drew a line in the snow the same shape as the tracks and made signs for walk, snow, and good.

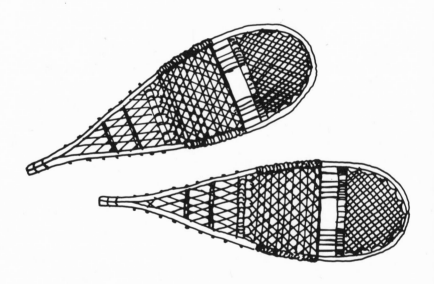

"Snowshoes," said Lone Hunter to Buffalo Boy. "I've heard of them but never saw any before."

"Where are they going?" Buffalo Boy asked.

Brave Elk pointed to the mountains and made the sign for mountain sheep by indicating the huge, curved horns. Lone Hunter watched the Cheyennes disappear. They were going high in the mountains on the snowshoes. If they can go where the mountain sheep stay, they can cross the mountains, he thought. That means we can, too, without ponies. But we mustn't make Brave Elk suspicious. He turned his back on the hunters.

"Let's go to the tepee and dry our moccasins," he said, touching his wet feet.

Later in the day he and Buffalo Boy met again and walked through the camp alone. "Lone Hunter, did you see how easily the Cheyennes walked on the snow?" Buffalo Boy asked. "If they hunt mountain sheep, they have to go all the way to the top of the mountain. Maybe we can still escape."

Lone Hunter looked up at the dark clouds drifting slowly toward the mountains. "Maybe we can," he said, "but don't show any interest in the snowshoes. We must learn how to use them somehow, but without the Cheyennes knowing it. If we leave we must be able to travel as swiftly as they do."

A few Cheyenne boys wore snowshoes, but Lone Hunter and Buffalo Boy did not see many in the entire camp. "Every warrior doesn't have them," said Lone Hunter. "There must be only one pair to each lodge. If we could steal all of them before we leave, they wouldn't be able to follow us. But that's probably impossible."

They watched the Cheyenne boys running over the snow, lifting their feet so the ends of the snowshoes trailed in the snow at each step. Brave Elk came out of the tepee with his father's snowshoes and offered them to Lone Hunter. He showed Lone Hunter how to tie the loose thongs over his feet, to hold the snowshoes fast, and the feet-apart, high-stepping stride that would carry him over the snow without falling. Lone Hunter tried the snowshoes, as if only to please his friend. He took a few steps to accustom himself to walking on snow. Satisfied, he pretended to run and tumbled awkwardly into a snowdrift. Brave Elk laughed, while Lone Hunter untied the snowshoes and handed them to Buffalo Boy to try. He shook his head, as if ashamed of his awkwardness, as if he never again would want to wear snowshoes.

After they returned the snowshoes to Brave Elk and he ran off to play with other Cheyenne boys, Lone Hunter and Buffalo Boy walked through the camp where the snow was trampled hard. A cold wind whistled through the winter lodges, and they held their robes tightly about them.

"We'll have to steal snowshoes," said Lone Hunter. "They're not easy to use, and we'll have to learn quickly. With them and some pemmican we should be able to cross the mountains. But we must go soon. Two Elks is still waiting for a chance to kill us, and more snow is coming. If the snow is too deep in the mountains we may lose the trail, and if a bad snow storm strikes us then we'll freeze. But we can't stay here."

The next day the air was still, and a few clouds seemed to hang motionless in the sky, shading the mountains from the sun. Cheyennes from other camps nearby came and squatted among the tepees. They eyed the Oglala boys curiously but without hostility. Using the Cheyenne words he had learned, Lone Hunter asked Blue Star about the visitors.

"Big dance, my son," she said. "Four days. Four is the sacred number of the Cheyennes." Lone Hunter nodded and smiled. This may be our chance to escape, he thought.

The first night of the dance the air was clear and cold. The Cheyennes built a huge fire in the center of the camp circle and danced to the songs of the drummers. Lone Hunter and Buffalo Boy watched until the broad white band of tiny stars, the Ghost

Trail, was high overhead. Yawning, they left the dance. Blue Star and Rainbow Woman smiled and said something in their language. As they returned to their tepees to wrap up in their robes for the night, Lone Hunter touched Buffalo Boy's arm.

"Did you hear what they said? It was something about Oglalas not being able to stay awake all night like Cheyennes. Tomorrow night we'll do the same thing, only we'll leave camp. We'll need snowshoes, heavy robes, some pemmican, knives, bows, and a few arrows. That's all we can carry. I think walking on snowshoes will tire our legs quickly until we're used to it."

"We won't be able to steal all the snowshoes," said Buffalo Boy. "It will be hard enough for us to get out of camp without being seen, the fire's so bright."

"No, we'll have to get far away before they miss us. If we get to the mountains first, we should be able to stay ahead of them."

As he lay down to sleep Lone Hunter listened to the hollow throbbing of the Cheyenne drums and the strange sounds of the songs. Soon he was asleep. Near morning he heard Blue Star and the other Cheyennes enter the lodge and roll up in their robes. They had danced all night. Lone Hunter lay still until he was sure they were asleep, then left the tepee.

He walked through the silent camp until he saw Buffalo Boy. Overhead clouds moved slowly before the rising sun. "It looks like another storm is coming, Lone Hunter. Do you still think we should try to escape tonight? It would be better to stay here and watch out for Two Elks than freeze to death in the mountains."

"We must try tonight. We may never have a better chance before spring, and Two Elks will kill us before then. Let's get the snowshoes and practice a little while no one is watching."

They slipped silently into their tepees and took the snowshoes from the stakes where they hung. At the edge of the camp they knelt to fasten the snowshoes on their feet. Buffalo Boy faced the camp, while Lone Hunter's back was turned to it. Buffalo Boy

stiffened and touched Lone Hunter's arm. "Back to your lodge quickly," he whispered. "Don't ask why."

Lone Hunter picked up the snowshoes and hurried to the tepee. Before entering it he glanced quickly around the camp circle. The hair on the back of his neck rose, and he felt a wave of terror sweep over him. Two Elks stood at the entrance of his tepee, bow and arrows in hand.

During the rest of the day Lone Hunter saw Buffalo Boy only from a distance. When Blue Star awoke, he helped her gather wood for the fire, wearing Yellow Bear's snowshoes. He worked

hard at breaking the dry branches and carrying them to the dance circle. When night came he was exhausted, but he had learned to manage the snowshoes fairly well.

Soon after dark the Cheyennes gathered once more for the dance. The old warriors struck sparks into the tinder, held it up to the Great Spirit, and lighted the fire. When it was blazing brightly, the drummers struck their drums, and the songs began. Lone Hunter wandered around the circle of dancers until he came to Buffalo Boy.

"When I touch my right ear, slip away to your tepee and get ready," he said. "I'll meet you at the big rock by the frozen pool."

Moving closer to the fire, Lone Hunter stood near it until his moccasins and leggings were dry. He saw Buffalo Boy move about the circle from time to time, not staying long in any one place. Good, he thought. When he leaves no one will miss him. He glanced about in search of Two Elks.

Standing with a group of young warriors watching the dancers was Two Elks. Lone Hunter frowned. If he was not dancing, Two Elks might miss them and discover their flight. Lone Hunter moved slowly about the circle, glancing at Two Elks from time to time. The dances went on for a long time without stopping and were interrupted only when the singers needed to rest their voices. Lone Hunter watched Two Elks and stamped his cold feet.

The singers finished their song and walked around the fire, stretching and warming their hands. When they returned to their places and began singing again, a line of young Cheyenne women danced toward the warriors. The warriors formed a line and danced to meet them, and the two lines moved forward and backward in the firelight. Two Elks was one of the dancers. Lone Hunter caught Buffalo Boy's glance and touched his ear.

Buffalo Boy backed slowly away from the circle and disappeared in the darkness. Rainbow Woman watched him go, then looked at Lone Hunter. He yawned broadly and let his head sag forward. Then without looking at her again, he walked wearily away from the firelight. Once in the dark Lone Hunter abandoned his pretended weariness and hurried to the tepee. He took a buckskin pouch from one of the stakes, filled it with pemmican, and tied it to his belt. He slipped his bow and quiver over his shoulder, drew his robe tightly about him, and took the snowshoes from the stake. Silently he pulled the tepee flap aside and peered out. For a moment he thought he heard the crunch of feet on snow, but the sound was drowned out by the Cheyenne songs, and he saw no one. Perhaps it was Buffalo Boy.

Lone Hunter stole from the tepee and around it away from the fire, toward the outer edge of the camp. Once beyond the second row of lodges, he turned south to the big rock near the pool. He was sure no one had seen him, but now the flight had begun he wanted to race for the mountains before they were missed.

The clouds grew heavier, and the air was ominously quiet save for the murmur of the drums and the whoops of the Cheyennes. From time to time snowflakes rested coldly on his face. He brushed them off and stared into the darkness. In the mountains it might be snowing heavily. If they were to cross the mountains before the snow lay higher than a Cheyenne tepee they must hurry. At any moment Two Elks might miss them and start in pursuit. Where was Buffalo Boy?

Buffalo Boy did not appear. Lone Hunter stamped his cold feet on the hard rock, scowled at the dark sky, and twice started back into the camp. What could be keeping Buffalo Boy? Had he been caught? If so, all was lost.

Lone Hunter slid down from the rock once more and started back toward the camp. He had gone only a few steps when he heard the soft crunch of footsteps in the snow. Quickly he flattened himself against the rock, out of sight. Buffalo Boy appeared, out of breath.

"Lone Hunter, Rainbow Woman came back to the lodge while

I was there. I pretended to be asleep when I heard her coming, but she seemed suspicious. She watched me a long time before she went back to the dance. If she looks again they'll know we've escaped. I'll go back and stay there. You go on without me. I'll try to delay them. Now go."

Lone Hunter did not hesitate. "Come," he said. "Let's get started. We'll stay together no matter what happens. Perhaps we can get across the mountains before they catch us; perhaps not. At least we'll take our chances together."

"But I have only a robe and snowshoes," Buffalo Boy protested. "I didn't have time to get pemmican or a bow. I'd better go back so you can escape."

"Put on your snowshoes," said Lone Hunter. "The Cheyennes would kill you at once if they knew I had escaped."

VI

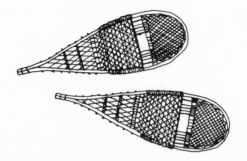

Tracks in the Snow

THEY PUT ON THEIR SNOWSHOES AND WRAPPED their robes closely about them. Lone Hunter pointed to the east. "The trail over the mountains should be in that direction," he said, "but since the camp was moved we have farther to go." He led the way, stumbling a little at first. Snowshoes are harder to use in the dark, he thought. He glanced back at their tracks. It looked like two bear cubs had been playing in the snow. It was a trail the Cheyennes could follow even in the dark. He shook his head and hurried on. There was no use trying to hide their tracks; only speed could save them. As they struggled away from the Cheyenne camp, the singing gradually died out in the distance.

In the darkness and snow all landmarks were hidden from sight

47

or so changed in appearance Lone Hunter could not be sure he recognized any of them. The swirling clouds hid the stars, so he did not have them to guide him. He stared hard into the night, hoping to see a hill or stone or tree that he recognized. They must find the trail to the low passes, or they would never get far over the mountains. But he saw nothing that seemed familiar.

As they crossed an open meadow and entered woods beyond, Lone Hunter stopped. "Do you think we're going in a circle?" he asked. "If we are we won't reach the mountains by morning."

Buffalo Boy breathed heavily a moment and stared into the darkness. "I can't tell," he said. "I don't think so. Let's keep going."

They struggled long through the snow. Lone Hunter's legs ached from having to lift his feet in the awkward snowshoe stride. He became more unsure of the right direction, more certain they were lost. Wearily he stopped on a hill to catch his breath. Buffalo Boy stood silently behind him. The wind blew gently from the south. Lone Hunter shook his head and rubbed his cold ears. Did he imagine it? "Listen!" he exclaimed. Buffalo Boy held his breath.

Far in the distance they heard faint sounds, difficult at first to recognize. They listened a moment longer. Lone Hunter felt his legs grow weak, and chills ran up his spine. Buffalo Boy clapped his hand over his mouth. He, too, recognized the sounds.

"Cheyennes singing," he said. "We must have gone in a circle. We're lost."

For a moment neither of them spoke again. Heavy snowflakes swirled about them, and the Cheyenne songs almost faded from hearing.

"Don't blame yourself, Lone Hunter," said Buffalo Boy. "It has happened to the best warriors. If they're still singing it means they haven't missed us. Let's go back to our tepees and try tomorrow night."

They turned in the direction of the singing, Buffalo Boy lead-ing the way. The sounds of the singing grew louder. Buffalo Boy stopped at the edge of a small stream.

"Lone Hunter! That must be a different camp. There wasn't any small stream near our camp. We may be lost, but we haven't gone in a circle."

He turned away from the camp and led the way toward where the mountains should be, until they could no longer hear the Cheyenne songs. The snow fell so heavily about them they could barely avoid walking into trees. Lone Hunter looked at their tracks. They were filling rapidly with snow.

"Wait," he called to Buffalo Boy. "We can hide now, and go on in the morning. Out tracks will soon disappear, and the Chey-ennes will lose our trail. They'll get to the mountains ahead of us, and we'll have to wait till they give up and go back to camp. I'd rather keep going and get out of their lands, but we're lost. We must wait for daylight to see where we are. Follow me."

He led the way under the sagging branches of a fir tree, sliding in carefully so as not to dislodge the snow. Buffalo Boy followed. Under the tree was a springy bed of fir needles, dry and sheltered from the snow. He and Buffalo Boy rolled up in their robes and slept.

Lone Hunter awoke. Something had disturbed him, but what it was he did not know. He looked up at the fir limbs over his head. Light was shining through. At his side Buffalo Boy still slept. He touched Buffalo Boy's shoulder. His companion opened his eyes and yawned. Lone Hunter held his finger to his lips for silence. Buffalo Boy opened his eyes wide and raised him-self on one elbow. Lone Hunter slipped out of his robe.

"I'm going to have a look," he said. "I think I heard something."

He climbed carefully up the huge trunk of the fir tree, resting his weight gently on the limbs. Near the top he peered out through an opening in the limbs. In a moment he slid down.

"What did you see, Lone Hunter?"

"A party of Cheyennes passed just north of us. I counted seven. Two Elks was leading them. Remember that rock that looked like a tepee? They went past it. We're not far off the trail after all. But

now we'll have to wait for them to return. We can't move or we'll leave a trail, and they're sure to find it."

Buffalo Boy lifted the buckskin pouch of pemmican and they each ate a handful. "I wish I had gotten some, too," he said.

All day they waited and watched, taking turns sleeping and

watching from high up in the tree. It was Buffalo Boy who saw the Cheyennes return, just before dark. He crawled back down the tree to Lone Hunter.

"I saw them," he said. "They were heading for their camp. They've given up."

"Did you see Two Elks?"

"No, Lone Hunter. He wasn't with them. I counted only five."

They sat on their robes and looked at each other for a moment. "He and one other warrior are still looking for us," said Lone Hunter. He shivered.

Buffalo Boy arose and, leaning low to avoid the limbs, peered out into the growing darkness. "It's snowing again," he said. "We can move closer to the mountains, and the snow will cover our trail."

They slipped out from under the tree and put on their snow-shoes. Heavy snowflakes fell about them, and soon it was so dark Lone Hunter drew an arrow from his quiver, and each held an end of it so they would not become separated. Before the middle of the night they stopped and again found shelter under the limbs of a fir tree. Each ate a handful of pemmican and then rolled up in his robe to sleep.

When they awoke Lone Hunter climbed the tree. He hurried down to Buffalo Boy. "The snow stopped too soon last night. I can still see our tracks. We can't stay here, but Two Elks must be watching the trail into the mountains. We'll have to circle behind them."

VII

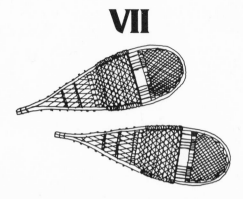

The Mountain Trail

THEY CRAWLED OUT FROM UNDER THE FIR TREE and looked long at the cliffs and canyons at the foot of the mountain. Buffalo Boy pointed to a dark line at the right of a cliff.

"There's where the trail came down," said Buffalo Boy. "If they're watching the trail they must be on top of that cliff above it."

"That's where they should be," Lone Hunter agreed. "If we can get into the canyon on this side of the cliff maybe we can get above them and reach the trail beyond where they're watching it. They can't see into the canyon, at least not to that ledge. Let's go, but keep out of sight."

Crouching behind trees, they reached a ravine leading to the canyon. Frequently they stopped and listened for sounds of the Cheyennes and glanced in all directions for the telltale tracks of snowshoes. They saw only the tracks of deer and elk, wolves and coyotes.

Near the canyon Lone Hunter stopped. He threw himself under a tree, and Buffalo Boy slipped in beside him. "What is it, Lone Hunter?" Buffalo Boy whispered.

"Watch. I think I heard someone."

They peered out through the branches, scarcely breathing. Two Elks came into sight, a bowshot away, between them and the mountain. His robe was drawn tightly about his shoulders, but in one hand he carried his bow, strung and ready for use. His eyes darted swiftly over the snow.

"He's probably going to make a big circle and look for our trail," Buffalo Boy whispered. "When he comes back he's sure to find it."

They watched Two Elks disappear from sight, moving swiftly along on his snowshoes.

"The other warrior must be up there watching the trail," said Lone Hunter. "He or Two Elks is sure to see us before long. We must hurry."

They slid down into the canyon and slipped off their snow-shoes to walk on the bare stone. Slipping an arm through the snowshoe thongs, they climbed to the ledge, and followed it along the side of the cliff, far up the canyon. It rose gradually away from the canyon floor. Near the top of the cliff it narrowed down to the width of Lone Hunter's hand. He stopped.

"Do you think we can make it?" he asked. "It's so close to the top I'd hate to have to turn back now. But it's a long fall from here."

They looked down at the rocky canyon floor far below and clung to the rock, shivering at the thought of falling so far. The wind moaned through the canyon, tugging at their robes. For a moment they gazed at the narrow ledge tapering off toward the top of the cliff.

From behind them, in the trees beyond the mouth of the canyon, came Two Elks' shrill war whoop.

"He's found our trail," said Lone Hunter. "Come on. We may as well fall as have him find us here. He'll lose our tracks on the rocks, but he will guess which way we had to go." He clung to the cliff and slid his feet along the narrow ledge. The cold wind whined about him, and he thought of the dizzying drop below. Not daring to look down, he kept his eyes on the top of the cliff and crept forward. Finally he reached a jagged rock at the top of the cliff and pulled himself up. In a moment Buffalo Boy was beside him. The air was cold, but they wiped perspiration from their faces.

To their right was a grove of stunted pines and firs, shielding the rest of the cliff from sight. "The Cheyenne scout must be out there, beyond those trees, watching the trail below," said Lone Hunter. "We can reach the trail over here, above him. I hope he keeps watching in the wrong direction for two days."

Skirting the trees they reached the trail and started toward the summit, where the trail crossed into the valley beyond. Snowdrifts lay over the trail in sheltered places, and the whistling wind cut and carved them like huge boulders. The boys climbed steadily upward, sometimes crawling over the drifts, stopping only now and then to look behind them for signs of the Cheyennes.

"Two Elks is trying to follow our tracks into the canyon," said Buffalo Boy. "He'll lose our trail on the rocks. That'll give us a little more time, but we must hurry."

They went on, fighting their way over the snow, on up the trail. Trees shielded them from sight until they neared the summit, where the trail ran across loose rock. Buffalo Boy stopped by a tree, breathing heavily. "We'll have to hurry across the open place," he said. "If they're watching they'll see us. I hope they're still looking in the canyon."

Gasping for breath in the thin mountain air, they waited a few moments longer. Bare rocks stood out of the snowbanks, and the wind sent powdery snow like fine spray into their faces. With a final look below, they pushed their way over the drifts toward the summit, driving their weary legs. In the west the sun lay near the horizon. Soon it would be dark.

They staggered the last few steps to the summit, lungs bursting from the effort. Lone Hunter leaned against a bare rock, while

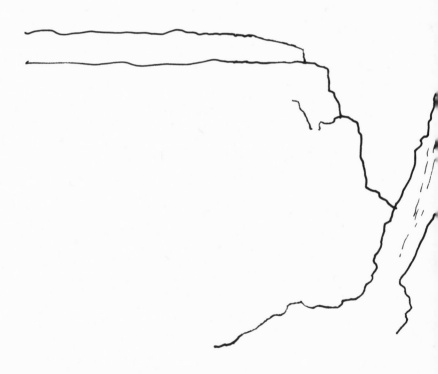

the screaming wind tore at his robe and drove snow into his face so hard he had to shield his eyes with his hand. He glanced back down the mountainside toward the cliff far below. Faintly he heard war whoops.

"Lone Hunter, they've seen us too soon. They're coming. What can we do?"

"Keep running," said Lone Hunter. He turned and ran down the trail toward the valley below, his legs trembling with weariness and terror. Two Elks and his companion were coming fast. They want us to know they're coming, Lone Hunter thought. They want us to be terrified, frightened nearly to death when they catch us. Behind him he heard the labored breathing of Buffalo Boy and knew that he, too, was terrified and exhausted.

Snow began to fall, lightly at first, but soon heavily. The mountain ahead faded from sight; the valley below was already dark. Lone Hunter and Buffalo Boy staggered down the trail, biting their lips and forcing their aching legs to keep going.

They reached the valley floor and stopped, staring into the darkness and blinding snow for some sign of the trail up the mountain ahead. "This is where we camped with the Cheyennes the last night," Lone Hunter gasped.

"I could lie down here and sleep forever," said Buffalo Boy. "Which way does the trail go from here? I'm so tired and scared I can't remember anything except that there weren't any good landmarks. Do you remember anything at all that will help?"

Lone Hunter strained his eyes staring into the darkness, seeing nothing, trying to remember the mountainside by daylight. "All I know is that I looked hard and saw nothing. But there was something here, if I can only remember it."

Wearily they started up the mountainside, feeling their way blindly. Lone Hunter slipped and fell.

"There's no trail here," he said. They went back to the valley, where they had camped with the Cheyennes. For a moment they stood, breathing heavily, trying to remember where the trail started up the mountain.

From the dark came the murmur of voices, and Lone Hunter slipped the bow from his shoulder and strung it.

"Two Elks can't be that near yet," he said. "We came down the mountain faster than they could climb it. But what are those voices?"

"The wind in the trees," Buffalo Boy answered.

"That's what I was trying to remember! There was a big pine near the trail. When the wind blew through it, it sounded like people singing or talking. Remember?"

They listened again for the sound and started up the trail past the murmuring pine. Slowly they struggled up the mountain, pulling their robes over their faces to keep out the driving snow.

The turning trail was difficult to follow, but where the snow had blown thin they could find it. They struggled on, far into the night. As they neared the top of the mountain, the snow lay heavily on the steep slope. The boys stumbled into the snow-laden limbs of a dwarf fir tree.

"We're off the trail," said Lone Hunter. "I can't follow it any more. If we miss that narrow pass, we'll never get over the mountain. We'll have to wait till daylight."

They crawled under the tree and with numb fingers scraped nearly level beds. The gnarled tree gave little protection, and wind and snow whipped over them. "The first one awake, wake up the other," said Buffalo Boy. "They can't find us before morning." Lone Hunter groaned in reply. In a moment they both were asleep.

VIII

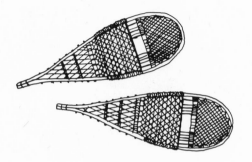

In the Cave

LONE HUNTER AWAKENED, AND OPENED HIS EYES narrowly. It was not yet dawn, but he could see his frosty breath floating up like a prairie mist. He rubbed his eyes, yawned, and stretched his aching muscles. He felt like rolling over and sleeping all day. He glanced up at the limbs of the fir tree forming a ceiling above his head and then at Buffalo Boy sleeping near his side. Sitting up, he nudged Buffalo Boy who also sat up, rubbing his eyes.

"I could go on sleeping forever," said Buffalo Boy. "I dreamed I was a bear, sleeping the Long Sleep. I was just getting started and hated to wake up so soon."

"Come," said Lone Hunter. "We must go." Each ate a mouthful

of pemmican, then shook the snow from his robe. They slipped out from under the tree into the semidarkness.

It was no longer snowing, but their tracks from the night before were already nearly filled. They looked down the mountainside but could not see far into the dark valley. Somewhere down there Two Elks and his companion were probably waking up, getting ready to resume the chase. They looked up at the mountaintop, already growing visible in the early morning light. The line of peaks and boulders looked the same in either direction.

The boys fastened on their snowshoes and drove their aching legs up the mountain, over the heavy drifts in search of the trail. It was Buffalo Boy who found it.

"Lone Hunter," he said. "See that faint line in the snow. The trail must be under it. I remember it made a turn like that just below the pass! Come."

They hurried up the trail, stumbling over the heavy drifts. Lungs bursting, they reached the narrow pass and stopped for a moment to rest. Beyond the pass the trail led down the mountain, into the foothills and the plains of Oglala country.

From below them on the trail came Two Elks' shrill war whoop. The two Cheyennes were striding rapidly up the mountain, crossing an open space below the summit. Lone Hunter and Buffalo Boy plunged into the pass through the rocks, struggling over the drifts, gasping for breath. As they came through the pass, the sun came from behind a cloud. Ahead in the distance beyond the foothills they saw the rolling plains of Oglala land.

As they ran down the trail Lone Hunter tried frantically to think of some way to elude Two Elks. Just a short delay would give them time to reach their own hunting grounds, where the Cheyennes would have to give up the pursuit. But Two Elks was close behind and gaining fast. He would surely catch them before they could reach the foothills.

Lone Hunter ran on, forcing his weary, trembling legs to carry him rapidly down the mountain. He heard the whistling gasps of Buffalo Boy at his ear. We can't go on much longer, he thought. And our own country is so near. As he ran he slipped his bow from his shoulder and tried to string it, but his arms were too weak, and he could not stop to place one end against the ground. He felt like throwing it away, but held it in one hand.

Two Elks and his companion whooped loudly when they reached the summit and began running down the trail. They were in plain sight now. His shout was triumphant, for his prey was in reach at last. That's how he'll sound when he lifts our scalps, Lone Hunter thought, driving himself down the mountainside as fast as he could go.

Ahead rose a rocky crag, and Lone Hunter slowed down. That was where the Cheyennes had stopped to drink at a spring, where the bear had come from a cave and frightened them off. He ran to the rock near the cave and slipped off his snowshoes.

"Come on," he said to Buffalo Boy. "This is our only chance."

"But, Lone Hunter. The bear. What'll we . . . ?"

"Follow me. I'll show you." Lone Hunter stepped silently into the black entrance of the cave, feeling his way along the wall, straining his eyes to see in the dark interior. The musky odor of the sleeping bear filled the cave. Lone Hunter heard its quiet breathing directly ahead. It was still asleep.

The wall seemed to go straight back towards the bear. Lone Hunter moved to the other wall, which curved sharply to the left. He followed it away from the opening, into total darkness. The cave seemed large, though he could not see how far it went. He reached up the wall. It slanted back toward the roof of the cave, and several small ledges ran along it. "Up here," he whispered to Buffalo Boy.

Climbing carefully, Lone Hunter mounted the sloping wall until his head touched the roof of the cave. By bracing his feet on narrow ledges he could sit back against the wall, facing the back of the cave where the bear lay. Buffalo Boy perched beside him. "If we have to sit here long," said Buffalo Boy, "our legs will give out."

As their eyes became accustomed to the darkness, they saw dimly the huge bulk of the bear at the back of the cave. It was curled up, head on its paws, sleeping soundly. Lone Hunter glanced down to the floor of the cave. "I don't think old Rota War-ank-xica can reach us up here. I hope not, for he'll be angry if he's awakened."

"Do you think Two Elks will come in after us, Lone Hunter?"

"I don't know. He wasn't with the war party that captured us, so he may not know the bear's in here. He'll probably come in. Help me string my bow."

Together they strung the bow, and Lone Hunter drew an arrow from his quiver. Two Elks' war whoop echoed through the mouth of the cave. The bear stirred, while Lone Hunter and Buffalo Boy shivered. Lone Hunter placed the arrow on the bowstring and waited. Buffalo Boy drew his flint knife and crouched against the wall, ready to spring. They heard the Cheyennes' footsteps rattling over loose stones at the mouth of the cave.

IX

The Bear Attacks

THE SHADOWS OF THE TWO CHEYENNES DARK-
ened the entrance of the cave, and as he heard their soft tread
Lone Hunter raised his bow. The shadows disappeared. Outside
he heard the sound of tree limbs breaking.

"What're they doing?" Buffalo Boy whispered.

"Probably making clubs. They'll be back soon, so be ready to
fight for your life."

They waited, their muscles cramped from clinging to the narrow ledges on the slanting wall, their toes numb from gripping
the rock. From the back of the cave came the sound of the bear's
even breathing. It still slept.

Once more the Cheyennes' footsteps echoed softly in the nar-

row entrance of the cave. Again Lone Hunter raised his bow and aimed his arrow along the corner of the rock around which the Cheyennes must come. He held his breath and waited.

The entrance of the cave grew suddenly light. Two Elks or his companion had made a pine torch. The rays of the sputtering yellow light flickered over the walls of the cave and threw strange shadows into the corners. At the back of the cave the bear still slept, a bulky mass of dark gray fur. Lone Hunter gripped his bow so tightly his cold fingers ached. Buffalo Boy still crouched beside him, knife in hand, ready to spring.

The end of the torch came into sight around the corner of the cave and then drew back. "There's a bear," the boys heard Two Elks whisper. "Don't wake it."

Lone Hunter slipped the arrow from his bowstring and knocked the flint arrowhead from its notch. He placed the blunted arrow on his bow and drew the bowstring back. He had the arrow aimed at the sleeping bear when the torch reappeared around the corner of the cave.

"They're back in this direction somewhere," Two Elks whispered to his companion. "You hold the torch while I use my bow."

In a moment Two Elks would be in sight. Lone Hunter released his bowstring, and the arrow flew toward the sleeping bear. Two Elks laughed when he heard the bowstring's hum. "They missed us," he said. "They're scared to death."

Lone Hunter watched the bear. It stirred uneasily, trying to wake up. It raised its huge head and saw the light, as Two Elks and his companions stole around the corner of the cave. With a deafening roar the bear leaped to its feet and rushed at the startled Cheyennes. For a moment the torch did not move, as Two Elks and his companion froze with surprise. Then screeching with fright they ran for the mouth of the cave. The light disappeared, and the cave was dark once more. Lone Hunter heard the bear growling and snapping and the cracking of bone or wood. There was a sound of scuffling, and the Cheyennes moaned.

"Old Rota War-ank-xica is angry," Lone Hunter whispered. "He mustn't find us. Even if he can't reach us, he probably wouldn't let us escape."

The bear's growls grew closer, and they heard it shuffling back into the cave, its huge claws clicking over the cold stone floor. It sniffed the place where the Cheyennes had stood, and the walls where they had leaned. Its throaty growls echoed loudly through the cave. Lone Hunter felt the hair rise on the back of his neck. At any moment the bear might be clawing at them, trying to climb the wall. He held his breath.

The bear sniffed and growled again and faced the entrance of the cave, baring its teeth. Then it turned and padded to the back of the cave, grumbling like a lame old warrior on a frosty morning. It sniffed Lone Hunter's arrow which had awakened it and snapped the slender shaft in its teeth like a straw. Still grumbling and growling, it circled its bed three times and lay down. Sucking its paws and still growling occasionally, it finally fell asleep.

Lone Hunter and Buffalo Boy clung silently to their perch on the sloping wall of the cave. Buffalo Boy wiped his moist hands on his robe. Lone Hunter lay his bow on the rock beside him and flexed his cramped fingers. Still trembling, they waited and watched the bear. It did not stir again.

"Let's get out before it wakes up again," Lone Hunter whispered. "I don't think Two Elks can harm us now." They lowered themselves gently to the cave floor and glided along the wall toward the entrance of the cave, ready to run at any sound from the bear. The bear made a growling, grumbling sound in its throat. The boys dashed out of the cave.

At the entrance they stopped and shielded their eyes from the brilliant light reflected off the snow. The sun was shining, and only a few clouds were in sight.

"Grandfather Sun, we're happy to see you," said Lone Hunter. "Where are the Cheyennes?"

Two broken bows and the remains of four battered snowshoes lay near the mouth of the cave. Bits of torn buffalo-skin robes were scattered about. Buffalo Boy looked down toward the spring.

"I see them, Lone Hunter," he said. "They're stretched out on that rock near the spring. Look at their wounds. We don't need to fear them now."

Lone Hunter laid an arrow on his bowstring, and they walked slowly toward the two Cheyennes. Beyond them the sun shone brightly on the foothills and prairies of Oglala land. The boys looked at the hunting grounds of their people and smiled. "I wasn't sure we'd ever see our own country again," said Lone Hunter.

Two Elks and his companion raised themselves weakly on their elbows. Like trapped animals they watched helplessly as Lone Hunter and Buffalo Boy approached. Two Elks opened his torn robe and bared his chest. Across it were long red gashes from the bear's teeth and claws.

"He's telling you to go ahead and shoot him," said Buffalo Boy. "They're helpless, and they think we're going to kill them. Without snowshoes they can't get back across the mountains anyway."

Lone Hunter stopped and lowered his bow. "Buffalo Boy, do you still hate the Cheyennes?" he asked.

"No, I don't hate them any more. They're not like I thought. Rainbow Woman was good to me, and so were some of the others."

"Let's give them our snowshoes. We don't need them any more, for we'll soon be out of the mountains. And they can't return to their camp without them."

He slipped his bow over his shoulder and clasped his hands in front of his body in the sign for peace, then made the signs for Oglalas and Cheyennes. Two Elks and his companion stared at him without replying. Lone Hunter and Buffalo Boy laid their snowshoes on the rock and turned down the trail.

Only once they stopped to look back. The two Cheyenne warriors were standing weakly by the snowshoes. When Lone Hunter and Buffalo Boy looked back, both warriors clasped their hands before them in the sign for peace. The boys waved in reply and hurried on down the trail.

X

The Strange Camp

AT DARK LONE HUNTER AND BUFFALO BOY
stopped in the foothills and crawled away under a tree for the
night. Little snow lay on the ground, except for a few well-
shaded patches. The boys took off their moccasins and leggings,
which were soaked through from walking in the melting snow.

"I'm cold and hungry," said Lone Hunter. "We can make a fire
and get warm and dry, but we haven't much pemmican to eat.
Tomorrow we'll have to hunt."

They made a small fire under the tree and hung their moccasins
and leggings over low limbs to dry. Lone Hunter divided the last
of the pemmican, one handful apiece. They ate it slowly, making
it last as long as possible. When it was gone, Lone Hunter looked

at the buckskin pouch. "I could eat this, too," he said. "I'm as hungry as a bear after the Long Sleep."

Rolling up in their robes, they slept until morning. When they awoke, Lone Hunter looked once more in the buckskin pouch, hoping there was a little pemmican he had overlooked. He sighed and tied it to his belt.

"Let's get started," he said. "If we see any sign of deer we can stop and hunt. There should be some in these valleys and meadows, as long as no hunters are near."

By midday they reached the edge of the foothills and followed

a sheltered valley that led gradually to the prairie. Pine and fir and spruce grew in parts of the valley, surrounding grassy meadows where the snow had melted. As they walked through the trees Lone Hunter stopped and smelled the breeze. "Smoke!" he said. "There's someone camped near here. It can't be Oglalas, for our winter camps are far to the south. If they're not Oglalas, they must be enemies. Let's scout their camp."

They slipped into the woods, avoiding the stream where the beaver dams were. As they reached the edge of the trees, they saw a thin spiral of smoke rising beyond the treetops across an open meadow. Keeping in the trees, they circled past the enemy camp. They moved stealthily, listening for the telltale sounds of men.

The wind changed and blew from them toward the camp. "I hope they don't have dogs," Lone Hunter whispered. "If they catch our scent and start barking, they'll give us away. I wish the wind would change."

But the breeze kept on, blowing softly toward the camp. The stillness was broken by a pony whinnying. Lone Hunter and Buffalo Boy sprang behind trees. Lone Hunter dropped his bow and clapped his cold hand to his mouth in surprise.

"What's the matter, Lone Hunter?"

"That was . . . I'm sure that was my Gray Pony. Come, let's see."

They stole through the trees toward the column of smoke. In a meadow beyond the trees they saw two Oglala tepees and eight ponies grazing nearby. Gray Pony, head held high, ears alert, sniffed the breeze and whinnied again.

Red Eagle, Lone Hunter's father, ran from one of the lodges and looked at the pony, then in the direction he was looking. Lone Hunter and Buffalo Boy came out of the trees and ran across the clearing. Red Eagle shouted; Lone Hunter's mother and Buffalo Boy's mother and father hurried from the tepees.

"We've come back," Lone Hunter called loudly. "Buffalo Boy and I have escaped from the Cheyennes." The women laughed and cried, embracing their sons over and over again.

"We didn't know who you were and we were trying to avoid you," Lone Hunter said. "But Gray Pony caught our scent. Why are you here?"

"Your pony kept looking for you," said Red Eagle. "It seemed to know you would come back. We stayed here, waiting, hoping you would escape. Now we can all go on to the winter camp. What a feast the Oglalas will have when they see you two."

Typesetting by G & S, Austin

Printing and binding by Edwards Bros., Ann Arbor

Illustration by Paige Pauley, Fort Worth

Design by Barbara Jezek,
Whitehead & Whitehead, Austin